Tante Golda's Apricot Jam Cookies

You'll need:

1/2 cup sugar
1/2 cup butter
1 egg yolk

1 cup sifted flour
1/8 teaspoon salt
2 teaspoons vanilla extract
apricot jam (or other preserve of your choice)

Ask a grown-up to help you.

Preheat oven to 350°F. In a large bowl, combine butter and sugar until creamy. Add egg yolk and vanilla, beat well. Add flour and salt, mix thoroughly. Form walnut-size balls of dough with your hands. Place on a greased cookie sheet about 1" apart. Press each ball with your thumb to make a small well in the center of each cookie. Fill each depression with a small spoonful of jam. Bake for 15 minutes or until golden brown.

Tante Golda sometimes preferred to place an almond in each well. When she did this, instead of using 2 teaspoons of vanilla extract, she used 1 teaspoon of vanilla extract and 1 teaspoon of almond extract. Either way, they're delicious!

SIMON & SCHUSTER BOOKS FOR YOUNG READERS An imprint of Simon & Schuster Children's Publishing Division 1230 Avenue of the Americas, New York, New York 10020 Text copyright © 1997 by Elsa Okon Rael. Illustrations copyright © 1997 by Marjorie Priceman. All rights reserved including the right of reproduction in whole or in part in any form. SIMON & SCHUSTER BOOKS FOR YOUNG READERS is a trademark of Simon & Schuster. Book design by Paul Zakris. The text of this book is set in 14-point Stempel Schneidler. Printed and bound in the United States of America. First Edition 10 9 8 7 6 5 4 3 2 1

A NOTE ABOUT THE ART

The illustrations were painted in gouache on smooth watercolor paper (Winsor & Newton gouache, Arches 140 lbs. hot press watercolor paper). The paint is diluted and used transparently for backgrounds and layered with more opaque paint for foreground details. Textures are added with a variety of sponges and brushes.

LIBRARY OF CONGRESS CATALOGING-IN-PUBLICATION DATA
Rael, Elsa.
When Zaydeh danced on Eldridge Street / by Elsa Okon Rael ; illustrated by Marjorie Priceman.
p. cm.
Summary: While staying with her grandparents in New York City in the mid-1930s, eight-year-old Zeesie joins in the celebration of Simchat Torah and sees a different side of her stern grandfather.
ISBN 0-689-80451-2
1. Jews-United States-Juvenile fiction. [1. Jews-United States-Fiction. 2. Grandfathers-Fiction. 3. Torah scrolls-Fiction.]
I. Priceman, Marjorie, ill. II. Title.
PZ7.R1235Wh 1997
[E]-dc20 96-35045

When Zaydeh Danced on Eldridge Street

By Elsa Okon Rael ∽ ILLUSTRATED BY Marjorie Priceman

Simon & Schuster Books for Young Readers

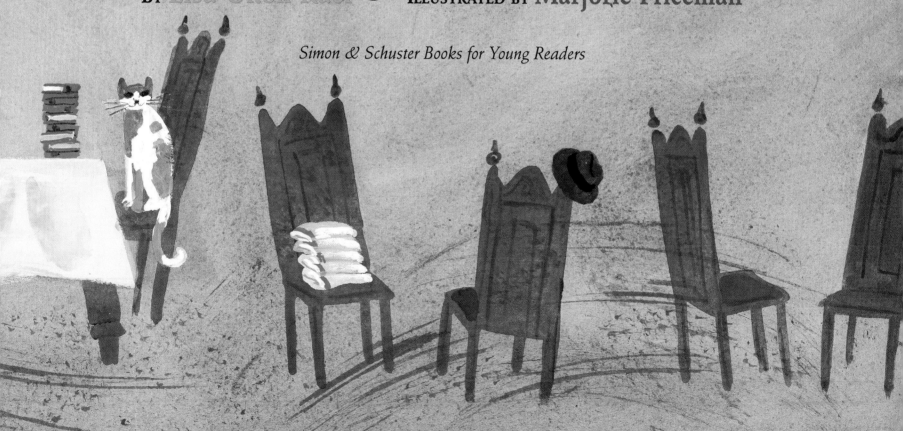

Zeesie wasn't really happy about the visit to her grandparents.

She didn't mind Bubbeh, whose sprightly movements and sparkling eyes always made Zeesie smile, but Zaydeh . . . well . . . to be truthful, Zaydeh didn't like children. Zeesie and all her cousins were afraid of him.

"Sit still and listen," he always ordered his grandchildren during his endless reading of the Haggadah at Passover seder. "Maybe you'll even learn something." And on Sukkos, he never allowed children into the festive booth in the backyard. "Children bring in dirt and make noise," he would say with a scowl, waving them away with the back of his hand.

But Zeesie couldn't escape today's visit, for Papa had to take Mama all the way uptown to the hospital on St. Marks Place to have a baby. "Tante Trina will bring you to Bubbeh Ruchel and Zaydeh Avrum," Papa explained. "You will behave?"

"Of course," Zeesie said with a frown. "I always do, Papa."

Teeny-tiny Bubbeh Ruchel greeted Zeesie and Tante Trina when they arrived at 17 Eldridge Street. "Come, my Zeeseleh, come in."

"So, Mama," Tante Trina said over her cup of tea, "what do you think they'll name the new baby?"

Zeesie had heard this discussion many times before. She looked over to the slender top drawer of the chifforobe which held a trove of familiar treasures.

"Go, Miss Curiosity, open it." Bubbeh nodded her permission. It was all the invitation Zeesie needed. There were two tubes of Tangee lipstick; the round, peach-colored box of Coty face powder; a pair of rhinestone buckles with a gem missing from each. In a faded, brittle envelope was Mama's Seward Park library card. There were several letters from Europe in spidery handwriting, addressed to Mama and written in Yiddish; a receipt for salve dated 1927, the year of Zeesie's birth; a half-full bottle of Waterman's blue-black ink; a yarmulke . . .

Before Zeesie finished looking through the familiar trinkets and treasures, Zaydeh arrived. She slammed the drawer shut quickly, expecting he would disapprove.

Tante Trina rose hastily and kissed Zeesie. "Behave yourself," she whispered under her breath, and left.

I wonder if Tante Trina is afraid of Zaydeh too, Zeesie thought.

"So," Zaydeh began, without a single word of greeting, "you think you'll have a brother or a sister?"

Truly, Zeesie wished for a baby sister, but she didn't want to tell that to Zaydeh. "I don't really care, so long as it's healthy," Zeesie replied, repeating what she had heard many times.

"So, do you know what today is?" Zaydeh asked.

"A holiday?" Zeesie took a guess as her heart began to race.

"Yes," Zaydeh persisted. "But what holiday?"

"Last week was Sukkos," Zeesie remembered.

"But today? What is today?" Zaydeh insisted. Zeesie felt as if she were in the middle of a test without having done her homework. "Simchas Torah," Zaydeh answered impatiently. "And do you know what we celebrate?"

Zeesie's voice squeaked. "The Torah?"

"Yes, but what about the Torah do we celebrate? Think, think," Zaydeh demanded as he poked his forehead with his index finger, pointing to his brain.

Zeesie was quiet. Was that her heart she could hear thumping? "I'm sorry, Zaydeh, I don't know."

Zaydeh shook his head sadly at his granddaughter's ignorance. Then he said, "Today we complete the Torah reading for the year, roll it back, and begin all over again. And we make a party in shul to celebrate. Would you like to go?"

Zeesie looked down at her shoe. "With you?" she asked.

"Of course with me. Who else?"

"They won't mind if children come?" Zeesie asked, hoping he might change his mind.

"If I bring you, it will be all right. So, do you want to go or not?"

Zeesie bent over to pick a bit of lint off her stocking. "Yes, please," she replied.

"Good. It's settled," he said, as though to close a business deal.

The rest of the day Zaydeh read his siddur by the window's light, as he always did, wearing his jacket and hat indoors, his lips moving as he mouthed the words he read.

Zeesie went into the kitchen to help Bubbeh prepare dinner. Bubbeh let her peel potatoes, a task that Zeesie did well, and Bubbeh smiled with approval. As they bustled about Bubbeh said, "Listen, Zeeseleh, I know it's not easy for children to be with Zaydeh. I know. Be a little patient and you'll have a good time in shul tonight."

After they'd eaten, Zaydeh said,
"So come. It's time to go."

"Is it far?" Zeesie asked.

"No. It's right downstairs. Across
the street," Zaydeh said. "Its name
is K'Hal Adath Jerusalem, but
everybody calls it the shul on
Eldridge Street."

Zeesie had never seen so beautiful a synagogue. Her father's place of worship on Cannon Street was plain, and her other Zaydeh's synagogue on Pitt Street was even simpler. But here the last of the sunset sparkled through brightly colored glass windows. Reds, greens, yellows, lavenders, and blues filtered in and cast a magical light across the pews. Wood carved in intricate patterns decorated the entire room. Zeesie spun around. This looks like a palace, she thought, and here I am, in the middle, like a princess!

Over to the side, Zeesie saw a table covered with baskets of shiny apples, bowls of raisins and almonds, and trays of cookies and sliced cake. Even though she'd just finished dinner, her mouth watered. It looks like a real party, she thought.

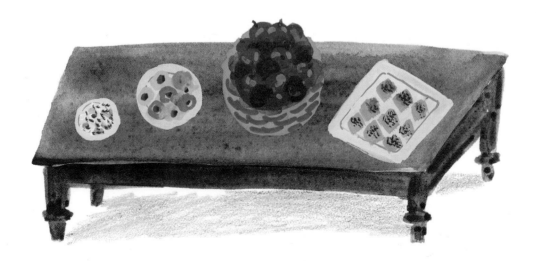

"Come! Take! Eat!" a man behind the table called to her and Zaydeh. There was loud laughter, singing, running, and for once, children were not being told to behave. Such sights and sounds! Zeesie stared, eyes open wide, at the children who streamed by her. She thought about mingling with them, but she didn't move.

Zaydeh walked away and joined two men on the bimah. Zeesie gazed as they silently rolled up the Torah, covered it with a velvet case, and placed it into the ark which slid open without a sound. The scroll was cradled in their arms like a newborn baby as they gently, gently placed it in a special dark cubby. They removed another Torah, slipped it from its cover, and carefully laid it on the lectern. They behaved toward the scroll as if it breathed with life.

"Come. Come, little ones. Onto the bimah," an old man said as he waved the chattering children to the small platform. Zeesie looked over to Zaydeh cautiously. He nodded to her, inviting her to join the giggling, squirming crowd, and she was happy to take her place with them.

As a large tallis was placed over their heads in blessing, Zeesie wiggled her way up to the front of the noisy group and stared at the scroll. She just had to see. This was the closest she'd ever been to a Torah. She had seen Hebrew lettering before, but this time she felt as though the writing held secrets, ancient sacred secrets.

When she left the bimah, Zeesie looked about for Zaydeh. She had a question.

Zeesie drew a deep breath. "Zaydeh? Please?" She gently tapped her grandfather's arm. "Can you tell me, Zaydeh, what is Torah? What does it mean? I know it's important, but why?"

"What?" Zaydeh's eyes popped wide open. "What? *What?*" Zeesie was about to repeat her question, but Zaydeh bellowed to one of the elders, "Did you hear that, Zalman?" To another he called, "Did you hear that, Beryl? My aynikle, my grandchild, asked me, 'What is Torah?'"

Had she done something wrong in asking? Zeesie stiffened in fear. But then, Zalman and Beryl smiled.

"You, my dear one," Zaydeh said, "have just asked a question with as many answers as there are Jews to answer it. The Torah is the writing of the five books of Moses. It was given to us by God in heaven to tell us how to live as Jews in this world." Zaydeh took a deep breath before he offered, in a whisper, "And would you like to know what I think? Personally?"

Zeesie tingled with curiosity. "Yes, please, please."

"Come closer."

Zeesie thought Zaydeh was about to whisper in her ear, but instead, as she leaned closer to hear him, Zaydeh kissed the top of her head.

"That's what I think is Torah. A kiss from God to the Jewish people to show His love."

A kiss from God! To Zeesie, these words were a warm embrace, not only from God, but from Zaydeh Avrum. He had never kissed her before.

Zeesie looked about the shul and saw grown-ups dancing and swaying with the children as they tenderly carried the Torah scroll in their arms and passed it from one to another. People kissed their fingers and reached out to touch the scroll.

"Simcha! Simcha! Simcha!" everyone chanted. Zeesie had never seen such joy, such freedom in a synagogue. And the sound! Zeesie bounced and swayed and turned along with the crowd. And then she saw—Zaydeh was dancing. *Zaydeh!* Imagine!

The doors of the shul burst open as though the place could
not contain so much happiness. Everyone followed as
Zaydeh, carrying the Torah, led the celebration dancing onto
Eldridge Street. Windows flew open and people leaned out to
clap their hands, call out greetings, and join in the singing.
"Simcha! Simcha! Simcha!"

As she paraded proudly next to Zaydeh, Zeesie thought of
her grandmother and looked up to the window. There she
was, tiny Bubbeh, waving and clapping her hands as if to say,
"See? I told you you would have a good time! See?"

When Zeesie and Zaydeh returned to Bubbeh, nearly breathless with excitement, there was Papa waiting with a big smile. "You have a baby brother," he told Zeesie.

"Mama is all right?"

"Mama is all right." Papa nodded and smiled.

"Chaim," Zaydeh said to Papa, "you should be proud."

"I am," said Papa.

"Yes, for the new baby, but also, also for your precious daughter. Of all my ayniklach, and Zeesie is the ninth, she is the only grandchild who has ever asked me about Torah. About its meaning, its essence. The only one. Do you know how rare it is, how remarkable, to have a child who wishes to know more? A child who asks? You have here a wonder."

"I know," Papa said, hugging his daughter. "I know."

And Zeesie knew she would always remember this perfect moment, clear as the sharpness of the beautiful black lettering on the white parchment scroll. The day had indeed been a simcha, a blessing. Zaydeh had called her a wonder. But there had been so many wonders that night. Zaydeh *dancing*—that had been a wonder! Her new baby brother was another. But most of all there was the Torah. Only the Torah could have made her stern grandfather kiss her, only the Torah could have made the people in shul dance and laugh and sing, full of love. The scroll was the most precious treasure of all, the wonder of wonders.

For Sol Rael, beloved husband, father, and Zaydeh.
—E. O. R.

Author's Note

The Lower East Side of Manhattan is rich with evidence of the Jewish immigrant experience of the 1930s. Snappy sour pickles can still be plucked from barrels of brine on Essex Street; pirogen (potato dumplings) are being served at Ratner's on Delancey Street, even after 97 years; bargains can still be found spilling out of the stores on Orchard Street; bialys (onion rolls) scent the air on Grand Street; and cafeteria tickets continue to be punched at Katz's Delicatessen on Houston Street.

These sights, smells, and tastes, bring back many memories of the time: dashing through frosty sprinklers on hot August days in Pitt Street Park; shivering on long lines on January Saturdays, waiting for the Seward Park Library doors to open for magical readings of fairy tales; and paying a nickel for triple-feature movie bills (Clara Bow, Tom Mix, and Charlie Chaplin) at the Glory Theater on Cannon Street.

Today, the old Eldridge Street synagogue is still stirringly beautiful, despite its unfortunate state of disrepair. Happily, the dedicated staff and volunteers of the Eldridge Street Project have assumed, as their mission, its restoration. Their healing efforts bring people of all faiths from everywhere to visit this beautiful United States landmark and to enjoy the flavor of its rich heritage.

—E. O. R.

Glossary

AYNIKLE, AYNIKLACH (AY-nick-ul, AY-nick-loch)—grandchild, grandchildren *(Yiddish)*

ARK—a closet where Torah scrolls are kept *(English)*

BIMAH (BEE-mah)—the platform in a synagogue from which the Torah is read *(Hebrew)*

BUBBEH (BUB-eh)—grandmother *(Yiddish)*

HAGGADAH (ha-GUD-dah)—a book read aloud at the Passover seder telling the story of the Jewish exodus from slavery in Egypt *(Hebrew)*

K'HAL ADATH JERUSALEM (kih-HAHL ah-DATH yih-ROO-shul-lum)—the name of the synagogue at 12 Eldridge Street on New York's Lower East Side, which literally means community of the people of Jerusalem *(Hebrew)*

PASSOVER—the eight-day holiday celebrating the Jewish exodus from slavery in Egypt 3200 years ago *(English)*

SEDER (SAY-dur)—the ceremonial Passover dinner during which the haggadah is read and symbolic foods are eaten in addition to the regular meal *(Hebrew)*

SHUL (SHOOL)—synagogue or temple *(Yiddish)*

SIDDUR (SID-ur)—prayer book *(Hebrew)*

SIMCHA (SIM-chuh)—celebration or joyful occasion *(Hebrew)*

SIMCHAS TORAH (SIM-chus TOE-ruh)—the holiday that celebrates the completion and beginning anew of the yearly Torah-reading cycle *(Yiddish)*

SUKKOS (SOOK-iss)—an autumn harvest holiday celebrated with the building of an outdoor booth, or tent, called a Sukkah (SOO-kah), in which prayer and festive meals take place *(Yiddish)*

TALLIS (TAHL-iss)—a shawl worn when praying *(Yiddish)*

TANTE (TON-teh)—aunt *(Yiddish)*

TORAH (TOE-ruh)—Jewish bible; the five books of Moses *(Hebrew)*

YARMULKE (YAHR-mul-kih)—skullcap traditionally worn by Jewish males *(Yiddish)*

ZAYDEH (ZAY-deh)—grandfather *(Yiddish)*

ZEESIE, ZEESELEH (ZEE-see, ZEE-sell-eh)—Sweet One, Sweet Little One *(Yiddish)*

Bubbeh Shayndel's Apple Cake

You'll need:

filling

5-6 apples, peeled and sliced
3/4 cup sugar
3/4 cup raisins
2 teaspoons cinnamon
1 1/2 tablespoons lemon juice

batter

1 cup sugar
3/4 cup oil
3 eggs
1 teaspoon vanilla extract
1 cup flour
2 teaspoons baking powder
1/8 teaspoon salt

Ask a grown-up to help you.

Preheat oven to 350°F. Toss together all filling ingredients (apples, sugar, raisins, cinnamon, and lemon juice) and set aside. In a large bowl, beat the eggs. Add sugar, oil, and vanilla. Mix thoroughly. Add flour, baking powder, and salt to the egg mixture and blend well. Pour 1/2 the batter into a greased 9" x 11" pan. Carefully place apple filling evenly over the bottom layer of batter. Pour remaining batter onto the apples. Bake for 50 minutes or until the top is golden brown.